MANJU'S WISHES

CHITRA SOUNDAR

ILLUSTRATED BY **VERÓNICA MONTOYA**

BLOOMSBURY EDUCATION
Bloomsbury Publishing Plc
50 Bedford Square, London, WC1B 3DP, UK

BLOOMSBURY, BLOOMSBURY EDUCATION and the Diana logo are
trademarks of Bloomsbury Publishing Plc

First published in Great Britain in 2019 by Bloomsbury Publishing plc
Text copyright © Chitra Soundar, 2019
Illustrations copyright © Verónica Montoya, 2019

Chitra Soundar and Verónica Montoya have asserted their rights under the Copyright,
Designs and Patents Act, 1988, to be identified as Author and Illustrator of this work

A catalogue record for this book is available from the British Library

ISBN: PB: 978-1-4729-5971-3; ePDF: 978-1-4729-5972-0; ePub: 978-1-4729-5973-7;
enhanced ePub: 978-1-4729-6950-7

2 4 6 8 10 9 7 5 3 1

Printed and bound in China by Leo Paper Products, Heshan, Guangdong

All papers used by Bloomsbury Publishing Plc are natural, recyclable products from wood grown
in well managed forests. The manufacturing processes conform to the environmental regulations of
the country of origin.

To find out more about our authors and books visit www.bloomsbury.com
and sign up for our newsletters

Chapter One

It was Mum's birthday. Manju wanted to give Mum a present. Cumin, Manju's cat, agreed.

Manju checked the toy box. "How about this crocodile?" she asked.

"Maybe the elephant? Perhaps the robot?"

Cumin wasn't sure about any of those.
He sprinted into Grandma's room.
Manju followed.

"We shouldn't be in here," she whispered,
"while Grandma is away on holiday."
Cats are allowed everywhere, thought Cumin.

Manju looked on the bed and under the
bed. She checked on the table and under
the table. But she couldn't find Cumin.
Then suddenly Cumin sprang on top of
Grandma's cupboard.
"Don't do that," said Manju. But it
was too late.

Chapter Two

The old cupboard rattled and wobbled and it came crashing down to the floor. A wooden box fell and something tumbled out.

It was Grandma's magic lamp. Manju picked it up and wondered if a genie still lived in there.

She tried to remember Grandma's instructions to make wishes.

Step 1: Put on a smile.

Step 2: Rub the sides of the lamp three times.

Step 3: Whisper the magic words: "*Jantar Mantar Jeeboomba!*"

Manju followed the steps and suddenly the windows shut, the room turned dark and a whiff of rainbow smoke rose from the lamp. She shut her eyes tight.

Chapter Three

"Good morning!"
Manju opened her eyes.
A genie smiled at her.
"Hello," said Manju.
"I've seven wishes
to spare," said
the genie.
"Want them?"
"Yes please,"
said Manju. She
was only expecting
three. Getting
seven wishes was
spectacular.

"Do you want some toys?" the genie asked.

"Not for me," said Manju. "I want to get Mum a birthday present."

"Go on then," said the genie. "Hurry up and make your wishes. I don't have all day. I'm working two lamps this week."

"I wish for the best
song ever," said Manju.
"Your wish is my command,"
the genie proclaimed.
A big noise erupted in the living room.
Manju ran downstairs to find out what
was happening.

A band, complete with drums, guitars and big speakers, had started to play rollicking music. This was not like the music Mum listened to. Even Cumin was hiding under the sofa.

"Mum won't like loud music," cried Manju. "I've changed my mind. I wish for the best book, please."

"I grant your second wish," said the genie, still playing on his air guitar.

Suddenly, a big book crashed in through the roof and pirates, giants and fairies jumped out of it.

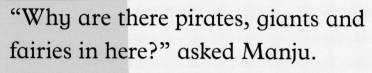

"Why are there pirates, giants and
fairies in here?" asked Manju.
"Because the best books always
have them," said the genie.
"But grown ups don't
read those kinds of books."

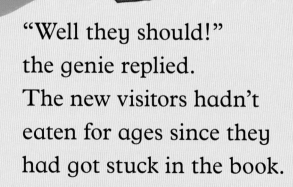

"Well they should!"
the genie replied.
The new visitors hadn't
eaten for ages since they
had got stuck in the book.

The pirates tore into some parathas and the giants gobbled up some ghee. The fairies sneezed a lot after sniffing the spice jars. *Even cats are better behaved than this*, thought Cumin.

"This is bad," said Manju. She had to find a different present.

Chapter Four

Manju shouted, "Mum loves everything about space."

"So what?" the genie shouted back.

"I wish for a spaceship," said Manju.

"Fine!" said the genie. "Here's a spacey third wish."

ZIP-ZAP-ZOOM!

A shiny spaceship landed and two
aliens with bobbing heads and runny
noses got out.
"They have runny noses," said Manju.
"It's the weather on Earth," said the genie.

"I wish you hadn't brought the aliens," said Manju. "They're rubbing snot everywhere."

Cumin nudged his bowl away from the aliens. *No snot for me, thank you!*

"What a waste of your fourth wish," said the genie and clicked his fingers.

The aliens took off and headed
back towards their own planet.
The giants jumped on the pirates.
The pirates charged at the
band. Cumin scuttled upstairs.
Everything was such a big mess
that Manju started to cry.

Chapter Five

The genie didn't know what to do.
"Please stop crying," he begged.
"I wish everything would go back to
normal," said Manju, sniffling.
"What a boring fifth wish," said the
genie. "But you must stop crying."
Manju nodded as she wiped her nose.

POOF!

The music stopped. The band, the
pirates, the fairies and the giants all
vanished. The roof was as good as new.
Everything returned to normal.

But Manju still didn't have a proper present for Mum.

"I wish I had an idea," she said. Cumin came back down the stairs. *An idea would be a good idea at this point*, he thought.

"A sensible sixth wish," said the genie, snapping his fingers.

Chapter Six

"Wait! No! That wasn't a wish," said Manju.

"Oops!" said the genie.

PING… An idea popped into Manju's head.

"Get me the sweetest sugars, the tastiest butter, the softest flour, the fluffiest eggs, the whitest icing, the creamiest cream and the darkest chocolate!"
"Your wish is my command," said the genie. "Seven wonderful things for the seventh wish."

"I wish for a recipe too," Manju shouted.
But the genie was gone. Cumin purred.
"Oh Cumin, I've run out of wishes,"
said Manju. "And I still don't have a
present for Mum."

Chapter Seven

When Mum returned from the garden shed, she was surprised to see all the stuff on the kitchen counter. "Hello, what's all this?"

Manju told Mum everything.

"Come here, you genie-stealer," said
Mum. "You've wished for wonderful
ingredients to bake a wonderful cake."
"But I forgot to ask for a recipe,"
said Manju.
"That's okay," said Mum.
"We'll figure it out."

Cumin growled and
sprang up onto the top of
the cupboards, just over
Grandma's cookbooks.
"Mum, look," said Manju.
"We can find a recipe in
Grandma's books."
Mum reached for
Grandma's old notebook.

Manju turned the pages until she found
a page labelled, "Recipe for the World's
Best Chocolate Cake".

"Perfect," said Manju.

Mum read the instructions while
Manju measured and mixed,
stirred and smoothed. Then Mum
put the cake in the oven.

Manju waited. Cumin waited too. Soon
the cake was ready.

"Now we have to let it cool," said Mum.
Manju waited. Cumin waited too. Soon
the cake was cool.
Then Manju wrote "Happy Birthday"
on the cake with the icing.

The H was a bit crooked. The B was too big. Still, Mum loved the cake.
"Happy Birthday, Mum!" said Manju.
"Thank you, my sweet," said Mum.
"And thank you, Cumin."
"Meow," said Cumin.